Tec and the Cake

Written by Tony Mitton

Illustrated by Martin Chatterton

Collins

Who ate the cake?

3

Was it the cat?

Was it the fish?

Was it the hamster?

Who ate the cake?

It was the dog!

Tec's Trail

Start

the cake

the cat

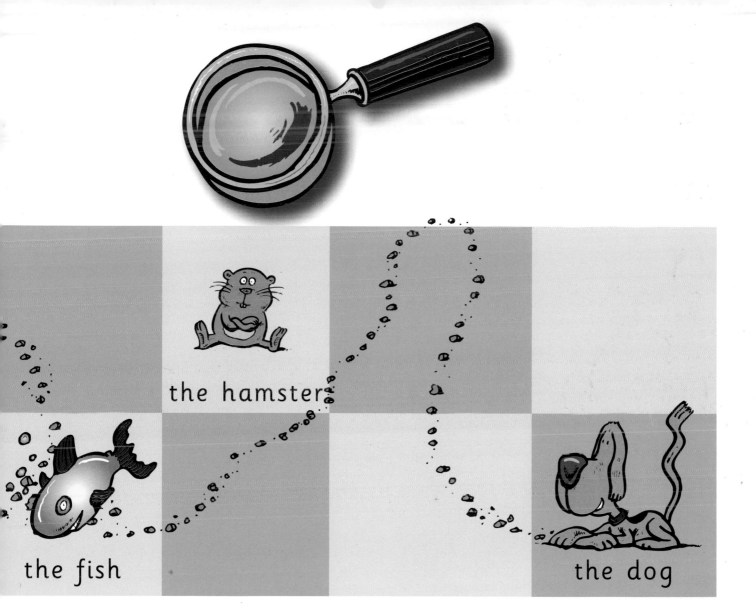

the hamster

the fish

the dog

Finish

15

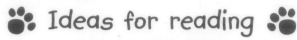

✿ Ideas for reading ✿

Written by Kelley Taylor
Primary Literacy Consultant

Learning objectives: tracking the text in the right direction; making one-to-one correspondences between written and spoken words; expecting written text to make sense and check for sense if it does not; reading on sight high frequency words; phoneme-grapheme correspondences c, f, h; retelling stories.

High frequency words: the, was, it, cat, dog

Interest words: who, ate, cake, hamster, fish

Word count: 24

Resources: small whiteboards and pens, two dice, counters, magnifying glass

Getting started

- Look at the cover together and introduce the character Tec. (Tec can also be found in two other Red level Collins Big Cat books: *Tec and the Litter* and *Tec and the Hole*.) Point out that Tec is a little word inside a big word – detective, which is what Tec is.

- Discuss what a detective does, and why he might use a magnifying glass (if possible show them a real magnifying glass).

- Look at the back cover and point out the blurb – this says what the story is about. Read the blurb together.

- Walk through the story up to p11, looking at the pictures, and ask the children to predict who they think ate the cake and give reasons why.

Reading and responding

- Ask the children to read the story aloud and at their own pace, pointing to each word as they read it. Encourage children to give their opinions on each suspect before they turn each page, e.g., *'I don't think it was the cat!'*

- Prompt the children to look at initial letters to help solve unknown words, reminding them that the pictures will help too.